D0558832

THE QUICK QUARTERBACK

STONE ARCH BOOKS
a capstone imprint

My First Graphic Novels are published by
Stone Arch Books — A Capstone Imprint
1710 Roe Crest Drive
North Mankato, Minnesota 56003
www.capstonepub.com

Library of Congress Cataloging-in-Publication Data
Lord, Michelle.
   The quick quarterback / by Michelle Lord; illustrated by
Steve Harpster.
      p. cm. — (My first graphic novel)
   Summary: Tigers' quarterback Andre is still recovering
from a broken arm—will he get his confidence back and
be able to win the big game?
   ISBN 978-1-4342-3281-6 (library binding)
   ISBN 978-1-4342-3861-0 (pbk.)
   1. Quarterbacks (Football)—Comic books, strips,
etc. 2. Quarterbacks (Football)—Juvenile fiction. 3.
Football—Comic books, strips, etc. 4. Football stories.
5. Self-confidence—Comic books, strips, etc. 6. Self-
confidence—Juvenile fiction. 7. Graphic novels. [1.
Graphic novels. 2. Football—Fiction. 3. Self-confidence—
Fiction.] I. Harpster, Steve, ill. II. Title. III. Series: My
first graphic novel.

PZ7.7.L67Qu 2012
741.5'973—dc23

2011032214

Art Director: Bob Lentz
Graphic Designer: Brann Garvey
Production Specialist: Michelle Biedscheid

Printed and bound in the USA.
002271

THE QUICK QUARTERBACK

written by
Michelle Lord

illustrated by
Steve Harpster

HOW TO READ A GRAPHIC NOVEL

Graphic novels are easy to read. Boxes called panels show you how to follow the story. Look at the panels from left to right and top to bottom.

Read the word boxes and word balloons from left to right as well. Don't forget the sound and action words in the pictures.

The pictures and the words work together to tell the whole story.

Andre loved football. He could throw the ball farther than most boys his age.

Coach Clark knew Andre was a hard worker.

But then Andre got hurt.

He broke his arm.

Six weeks later, Andre went back to the doctor.

He needed another X-ray.

Andre could play in the next football game.

Andre was excited to play football. But he was
nervous, too.

Andre tried to find someone to play catch with.
His brother was busy.

His mom and dad were busy.

Grandpa was not busy. But Andre did not want to bother him.

Andre went out to the backyard. He threw the ball up. His arm felt stiff.

Andre's dog, Zip, ran up to him. He tried to grab the football out of Andre's hand.

Andre aimed for the oak tree.

Zip snatched up the ball and ran!

Andre had not run much with his cast. Now,
chasing Zip was fun. They ran together every day.

Soon it was game day. The Tigers played the Tanks.

Andre threw a pass. The ball flopped. A Tanks player caught it.

The Tigers could not stop the player. He ran to the end zone. The Tanks scored six points.

Soon the score was tied. The Tigers waited for Andre to call the next play.

Andre did not know what to do. He was scared to throw. Finally he made a decision.

Andre was worried about his arm.

Andre faced the Tank's defense. They were huge!

The center snapped the football. Andre
grabbed it.

Nobody from Andre's team was open!

Then Andre saw Henry. Henry was open, but Andre could not throw far enough to reach him.

Andre thought about all of the practice he missed. Then he had an idea!

Andre ran toward the goal. The Tanks tried to stop him.

Andre ran zigzags like he had with his dog.
Playing with Zip was good practice after all.

He made it to the end zone. Touchdown!

The Tigers won the football game thanks to Andre, the quick quarterback.

BIOGRAPHIES

MICHELLE LORD lives in New Braunfels, Texas, with her husband, her three children, her two labradoodles, and her one dachshund.

STEVE HARPSTER has loved drawing funny cartoons, mean monsters, and goofy gadgets since he was able to pick up a pencil. Now he does it for a living. Steve lives in Columbus, Ohio, with his wonderful wife, Karen, and their sheepdog, Doodle.

GLOSSARY

CENTER (SEN-tur) — the player in the middle of a line who puts the football in play by passing it between his legs

DEFENSE (DEE-fens) — the team that does not have control of the ball

END ZONE (END ZOHN) — the end of the football field where a touchdown is scored

QUARTERBACK (KWOR-tur-bak) — in football, the player who leads the team by passing the ball or handing it off to a runner

SNAPPED (SNAPT) — to put a football in play by passing it between the legs

TOUCHDOWN (TUHCH-doun) — when the other team gets into your end zone and scores six points

DISCUSSION QUESTIONS

1. Andre broke his arm. Have you ever broken a bone? What happened?

2. How did Zip help Andre practice?

3. During the game, Andre saw that Henry was open. But he thought Henry was too far away. What do you think would have happened if Andre tried to throw to Henry?

WRITING PROMPTS

1. Pretend you are Andre's friend and he has just broken his arm. Make him a get-well-soon card.

2. Make a list of five words that make you think of football.

3. Draw a picture of your favorite part of this story. Then write a sentence to describe it.

MY FIRST GRAPHIC NOVEL

These books are the perfect introduction to the world of safe, appealing graphic novels. Each story uses familiar topics, repeating patterns, and core vocabulary words appropriate for a beginning reader. Combine the entertaining story with comic book panels, exciting action elements, and bright colors and a safe graphic novel is born.

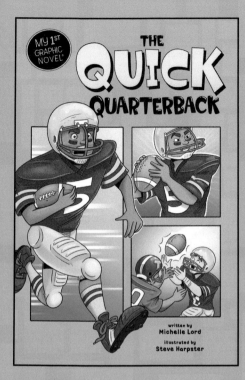

MY 1ST GRAPHIC NOVEL

THE
QUICK
QUARTERBACK

written by
Michelle Lord

illustrated by
Steve Harpster

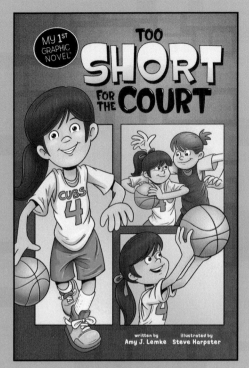

MY 1ST GRAPHIC NOVEL

TOO
SHORT
FOR THE COURT

written by
Amy J. Lemke

illustrated by
Steve Harpster

MY 1ST GRAPHIC NOVEL

THE
SWIM
RACE

written by
Anita Yasuda

illustrated by
Steve Harpster

MY 1ST GRAPHIC NOVEL

FIRST BASE
BLUES

written by
Anita Yasuda

illustrated by
Steve Harpster